For Lila, who loves rabbits,
especially hungry little ones.

This book is given with love

To:

_____

From:

_____

ISBN: 978-1-953177-92-6

Edition: January 2021

For all inquiries, please contact us at:
info@puppysmiles.org

To see more of our books, visit us at:
www.PuppyDogsAndIceCream.com

Hungry Little Rabbit

Martin Beckett

Early one morning,
a rabbit was hopping around...

when from his stomach
came the strangest sound.

"Oh my," said the rabbit.
"I'm hungry and beat,
I wonder if there is anything
around here to eat?'

He looked down to his feet
and then up to the sky,
then spotted a garden
and some lettuce to try!

So off he hopped
with a spring and a jump,
until he came to the lettuce
and chomped them right up.

The rabbit licked his lips and sighed,
"Lettuce just isn't for me,
I've eaten loads already,
but I'm still hungry!"

"Oh my," said the rabbit.
"I'm quite hungry and beat,
I wonder if there is anything
else I can eat?"

He looked down to his feet
and then up to the sky.
Then hopped over to some radishes
that had caught his eye!

So off he hopped
with a spring and a jump,
until he came to the radishes
and munched them right up.

"Radishes are nice,
but they're just not for me.
I've eaten so many,
but I'm still hungry!"

"Oh my," said the rabbit.
"I'm very hungry and beat,
There has to be something
more here to eat!"

GRRROOWWWL!

He looked down to his feet
and then up to the sky,
then spotted a field
he knew he couldn't pass by!

So off he hopped
with a spring in his tail,
until he came to a carrot
in the middle of the trail.

"Oh wow," said the rabbit.
"That's the biggest carrot I've seen,
and I'm so hungry
that it just might fill me!"

So, he took hold of the top,
gave it a tug and a huck,
but the carrot was too big
and it was much too stuck.

"Oh my," said the rabbit.
"I'm so hungry indeed,
but how can I get
this giant carrot freed?'

He looked down to his feet
and then up to the sky,
then spotted a spade
that he could use to pry!

So off he hopped
with a spring in his tail,
returning to dig,
but he was doomed to fail.

The rabbit panted and gasped,
"Digging is hard as hard can be,
surely this tiny spade
won't break this carrot free!"

"I'm incredibly hungry,"
the rabbit decreed,
"but how am I to get
this tasty carrot freed?"

He looked around swiftly,
and saw just the trick!
"I'll use the farmer's digger
to dig it up quick!"

So off he hopped
with a spring in his tail,
and returned in the digger,
but he wouldn't prevail.

Slowly the digger came to a stop
"Gas for this thing isn't free,
refueling this digger
is just not for me!"

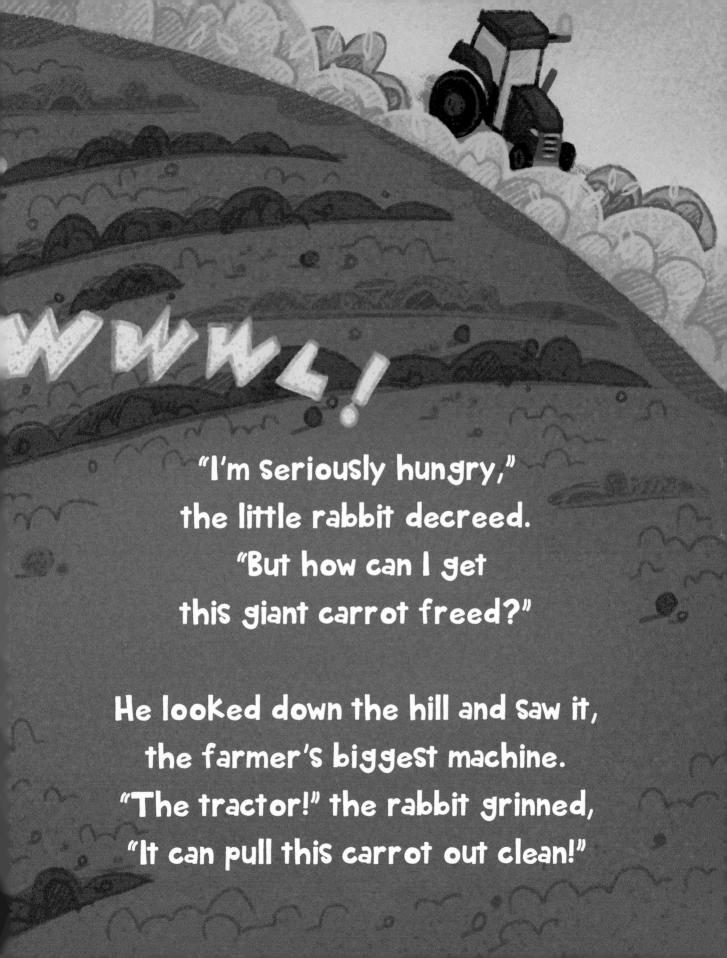

WWWL!

"I'm seriously hungry,"
the little rabbit decreed.
"But how can I get
this giant carrot freed?"

He looked down the hill and saw it,
the farmer's biggest machine.
"The tractor!" the rabbit grinned,
"It can pull this carrot out clean!"

So off he hopped
with a spring in his tail,
and returned in the tractor
which pulled to unveil
the giant carrot that growled
and started to romp...

then a

CHOMP,

CHOMP

CHOMP!

"That carrot was a monster!"
He smiled and licked his lips clean,
"Monstrously tasty,
and the biggest I've seen!
That monster carrot was just right for me!"

The no-longer hungry rabbit
patted his belly and walked home.

Until..."Oh dear, I'm hungry,"
he said with a groan.

The End

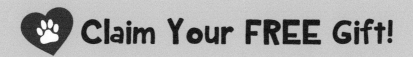 **Claim Your FREE Gift!**

Visit ➡ **PDICBooks.com/Gift**

Thank you for purchasing Hungry Little Rabbit,
and welcome to the Puppy Dogs & Ice Cream family.

We're certain you're going to love the little gift
we've prepared for you at the website above.